SCARY SÉANCES

SHORT STORIES OF SÉANCES AND VISITATIONS

British Library Cataloguing-in-Publication Data
A catalogue record for this book is available from
the British Library

Contents

Biographies of the Authors

The Rapping Spirits

The writer, who is about to record three spiritual experiences of his own in the present truthful article, deems it essential to state that, down to the time of his being favoured therewith, he had not been a believer in rappings, or tippings. His vulgar notions of the spiritual world, represented its inhabitants as probably advanced, even beyond the intellectual supremacy of Peckham or New York; and it seemed to him, considering the large amount of ignorance, presumption, and folly with which this earth is blessed, so very unnecessary to call in immaterial Beings to gratify mankind with bad spelling and worse nonsense, that the presumption was strongly against those respected films taking the trouble to come here, for no better purpose than to make super-erogatory idiots of themselves.

This was the writer's gross and fleshy state of mind at so late a period as the twenty-sixth of December last. On that memorable morning, at about two hours after daylight—that is to say, at twenty minutes before ten by the writer's watch, which stood on a table at his bedside, and which can be seen at the publishing-office, and identified as a demi-chronometer made by Bautte of Geneva, and numbered 67,709—on that memorable morning, at about two hours after daylight, the writer, starting up in bed with his hand to his forehead, distinctly felt seventeen heavy throbs or beats in that region. They were accompanied by a feeling of pain in the locality, and by a general sensation not unlike that which is usually attendant on biliousness. Yielding to a sudden impulse, the writer asked, "What is this?"

The answer immediately returned (in throbs or beats upon the forehead) was, "Yesterday."

The writer then demanded, being as yet but imperfectly awake, "What was yesterday?"

Answer: "Christmas Day."

The writer, being now quite come to himself, inquired, "Who is the Medium in this case?"

Answer: "Clarkins."

Question: "Mrs. Clarkins, or Mr. Clarkins?"

Answer: "Both."

Question: "By Mr., do you mean Old Clarkins, or Young Clarkins?"

Answer: "Both."

Now, the writer had dined with his friend Clarkins (who can be appealed to, at the State Paper Office) on the previous day, and spirits had actually been discussed at that dinner, under various aspects. It was in the writer's remembrance, also, that both Clarkins Senior and Clarkins Junior had been very active in such discussion, and had rather pressed it on the company. Mrs. Clarkins too had joined in it with animation, and had observed, in a joyous if not an exuberant tone, that it was "only once a year."

Convinced by these tokens that the rapping was of spiritual origin, the writer proceeded as follows, "Who are you?"

The rapping on the forehead was resumed, but in a most incoherent manner. It was for some time impossible to make sense of it. After a pause, the writer (holding his head) repeated the inquiry in a solemn voice, accompanied with a groan, "Who *are* you?"

Incoherent rappings were still the response.

The writer then asked, solemnly as before, and with another groan, "What is your name?"

The reply was conveyed in a sound exactly resembling a loud hiccough. It afterwards appeared that this spiritual voice was distinctly heard by Alexander Pumpion, the writer's footboy (seventh son of Widow Pumpion, mangler), in an adjoining chamber.

Question: "Your name cannot be Hiccough? Hiccough is not a proper name."

No answer being returned, the writer said, "I solemnly charge you, by our joint knowledge of Clarkins the

Medium—of Clarkins Senior, Clarkins Junior, and Clarkins Mrs.—to reveal your name!"

The reply rapped out with extreme unwillingness, was "Sloe-Juice, Logwood, Blackberry."

This appeared to the writer sufficiently like a parody on Cobweb, Moth, and Mustard-seed, in the *Midsummer Night's Dream*, to justify the retort, "*That* is not your name?"

The rapping spirit admitted, "No."

"Then what do they generally call you?"

A pause.

"I ask you, what do they generally call you?"

The spirit, evidently under coercion, responded, in a most solemn manner, "Port!"

This awful communication caused the writer to lie prostrate, on the verge of insensibility, for a quarter of an hour during which the rappings were continued with violence, and a host of spiritual appearances passed before his eyes, of a black hue, and greatly resembling tadpoles endowed with the power of occasionally spinning themselves out into musical notes as they swam down into space. After contemplating a vast legion of these appearances, the writer demanded of the rapping spirit, "How am I to present you to myself? What, upon the whole, is most like you?"

The terrific reply was, "Blacking."

As soon as the writer could command his emotion, which was now very great, he inquired, "Had I better take something?"

Answer: "Yes."

Question: "Can I write something?"

Answer: "Yes."

A pencil and a slip of paper which were on the table at the bedside immediately bounded into the writer's hand, and he found himself forced to write (in a curiously unsteady character and all downhill, whereas his own writing is remarkably plain and straight), the following spiritual note.

"Mr. C.D.S. Pooney presents his compliments to Messrs. Bell and Company, Pharmaceutical Chemists, Oxford Street, opposite to Portland Street, and begs them to have the goodness to send him by bearer a five-grain genuine blue pill and a genuine black draught of corresponding power."

But, before entrusting this document to Alexander Pumpion (who unfortunately lost it on his return, if he did not even lay himself open to the suspicion of having wilfully inserted it into one of the holes of a perambulating chestnut-roaster, to see how it would flare), the writer resolved to test the rapping spirit with one conclusive question. He therefore asked, in a slow and impressive voice, "Will these remedies make my stomach ache?"

It is impossible to describe the prophetic confidence of the reply. "*Yes.*" The assurance was fully borne out by the result, as the writer will long remember; and after this experience it were needless to observe that he could not longer doubt.

The next communication of a deeply interesting character with which the writer was favoured, occurred on one of the leading lines of railway. The circumstances under which the revelation was made to him—on the second day of January in the present year—were these: He had recovered from the effects of the previous remarkable visitation, and had again been partaking of the compliments of the season. The preceding day had been passed in hilarity. He was on his way to a celebrated town, a well-known commercial emporium where he had business to transact, and had lunched in a somewhat greater hurry than is usual on railways, in consequence of the train being behind time. His lunch had been very reluctantly administered to him by a young lady behind a counter. She had been much occupied at the time with the arrangement of her hair and dress, and her expressive countenance had denoted disdain. It will be seen that this young lady proved to be a powerful medium.

The writer had returned to the first-class carriage in which he chanced to be travelling alone, the train had resumed its motion, he had fallen into a doze, and the unimpeachable watch already mentioned recorded forty-five minutes to have elapsed since his interview with the medium, when he was aroused by a very singular musical instrument. This instrument, he found to his admiration not unmixed with alarm, was performing in his inside. Its tones were of a low and rippling character, difficult to describe: but, if such a comparison may be admitted, resembling a melodious heartburn. Be this as it may, they suggested that humble sensation to the writer.

Concurrently with his becoming aware of the phenomenon in question, the writer perceived that his attention was being solicited by a hurried succession of angry raps in the stomach, and a pressure on the chest. A sceptic no more, he immediately communed with the spirit. The dialogue was as follows:

Question: "Do I know your name?"

Answer "*I* should think so!"

Question: "Does it begin with a P?"

Answer: (second time): "*I* should think so!"

Question: "Have you two names, and does each begin with a P?"

Answer (third time): "*I* should think so!"

Question: "I charge you to lay aside this levity, and inform me what you are called."

The spirit, after reflecting for a few seconds, spelt out "P.O.R.K." The musical instrument then performed a short and fragmentary strain. The spirit then recommenced, and spelt out the word "P.I.E."

Now, this precise article of pastry, this particular viand or comestible, actually had formed—let the scoffer know—the staple of the writer's lunch, and actually had been handed to him by the young lady whom he now knew to be a powerful medium! Highly gratified by the conviction thus forced upon his mind that the knowledge with which he conversed was not of this world, the writer pursued the dialogue.

Question: "They call you pork pie?"

Answer: "Yes."

Question (which the writer timidly put, after struggling with some natural reluctance): "Are you in fact, pork pie?"

Answer: "Yes."

It were vain to attempt a description of the mental comfort and relief which the writer derived from this important answer. He proceeded:

Question: "Let us understand each other. A part of you is pork, and a part of you is pie?"

Answer: "Exactly so."

Question: "What is your pie-part made of?"

Answer: "Lard." Then came a sorrowful strain from the musical instrument. Then the word, "Dripping."

Question: "How am I to present you to my mind? What are you most like?"

Answer (very quickly): "Lead."

A sense of despondency overcame the writer at this point. When he had in some measure conquered it, he resumed:

Question: "Your other nature is a porky nature. What has that nature been chiefly sustained upon?"

Answer (in a sprightly manner): "Pork, to be sure!"

Question: "Not so. Pork is not fed upon pork?"

Answer: "Isn't it, though!"

A strange internal feeling, resembling a flight of pigeons, seized upon the writer. He then became illuminated in a surprising manner, and said, "Do I understand you to hint that the human race, incautiously attacking the indigestible fortresses called by your name, and not having time to storm them, owing to the great solidity of their almost impregnable walls, are in the habit of leaving much of their contents in the hands of the mediums, who with such pig nourish the pigs of the future pies?"

Answer: "That's it!"

Question: "Then to paraphrase the words of our immortal bard—"

Answer (interrupting): *"The same pork in its time, makes many pies, its least being seven pastries."*

The writer's emotion was profound. But, again desirous still further to try the spirit, and to ascertain whether, in the poetic phraseology of the advanced seers of the United States, it hailed from one of the inner and more elevated circles, he tested its knowledge with the following:

Question: "In the wild harmony of the musical instrument within me, of which I am again conscious, what other substances are there airs of, besides those you have mentioned?"

Answer: "Cape, Gamboge. Camomile. Treacle. Spirits of wine. Distilled potatoes."

Question: "Nothing else?"

Answer: "Nothing worth mentioning."

Let the scorner tremble and do homage; let the feeble sceptic blush! The writer at his lunch had demanded of the powerful medium, a glass of sherry, and likewise a small glass of brandy. Who can doubt that the articles of commerce indicated by the spirit were supplied to him from that source under those two names?

One other instance may suffice to prove that experiences of the foregoing nature are no longer to be questioned, and that it ought to be made capital to attempt to explain them away. It is an exquisite case of tipping.

The writer's destiny had appointed him to entertain a hopeless affection for Miss L.B., of Bungay, in the county of Suffolk. Miss L.B. had not, at the period of the occurrence of the tipping, openly rejected the writer's offer of his hand and heart; but it has since seemed probable that she had been withheld from doing so, by filial fear of her father, Mr. B., who was favourable to the writer's pretensions. Now, mark the tipping. A young man, obnoxious to all well-constituted minds (since married to Miss L.B.), was visiting at the house. Young B. was also home from school. The writer was present. The family party were assembled about a round table. It was the spiritual time of twilight in the month of July. Objects could not be discerned with any degree of distinctness. Suddenly, Mr. B., whose senses had been lulled to repose, infused terror into all our breasts, by uttering a passionate roar or ejaculation. His words (his education was neglected in his youth) were exactly these: "Damn, here's somebody a shoving of a letter into my hand, under my own mahogany!"

Consternation seized the assembled group. Mrs. B. augmented the prevalent dismay by declaring that somebody had been softly treading on her toes, at intervals, for half an hour. Greater consternation seized the assembled group. Mr. B. called for lights. Now, mark the tipping.

Young B. cried (I quote his expressions accurately), "It's

the spirits, father! They've been at it with me this last fortnight."

Mr. B demanded with irascibility, "What do you mean, sir? What have they been at?"

Young B. replied, "Wanting to make a regular Post-Office of me, father. They're always handing impalpable letters to me, father. A letter must have come creeping round to you by mistake. I must be a medium, father. O here's a go!" cried young B. "If I ain't a jolly medium!"

The boy now became violently convulsed, sputtering exceedingly, and jerking out his legs and arms in a manner calculated to cause me (and which did cause me) serious inconvenience; for, I was supporting his respected mother within range of his boots, and he conducted himself like a telegraph before the invention of the electric one. All this time Mr. B. was looking about under the table for the letter, while the obnoxious young man, since married to Miss L.B., protected that young lady in an obnoxious manner.

"O here's a go!" Young B. continued to cry without intermission. "If I an't a jolly medium, father! Here's a go! There'll be a tipping presently, father. Look out for the table!"

Now mark the tipping. The table tipped so violently as to strike Mr. B. a good half-dozen times on his bald head while he was looking under it; which caused Mr. B. to come out with great agility, and rub it with much tenderness (I refer to his head), and to imprecate it with much violence (I refer to the table). I observed that the tipping of the table was uniformly in the direction of the magnetic current; that is to say, from south to north, or from young B. to Mr. B. I should have made some further observations on this deeply interesting point, but that the table suddenly revolved, and tipped over on myself, bearing me to the ground with a force increased by the momentum imparted to it by young B., who came over with it in a state of mental exaltation, and could not be displaced for some time. In the interval, I was aware of being crushed by his weight and the table's, and also of his constantly calling out to his sister and the obnoxious young man, that he foresaw there would be another tipping presently.

None such, however, took place. He recovered after taking a short walk with them in the dark, and no worse effects of the very beautiful experience with which we had been favoured, were perceptible in him during the rest of the evening, than a slight tendency to hysterical laughter, and a noticeable attraction (I might almost term it fascination) of his left hand, in the direction of his heart or waistcoat-pocket.

Was this, or was it not, a case of tipping? Will the sceptic and the scoffer reply?

The Sire de Malétroit's Door
Robert Louis Stevenson

Denis de Beaulieu was not yet two-and-twenty, but he counted himself a grown man, and a very accomplished cavalier into the bargain. Lads were early formed in that rough, warfaring epoch; and when one has been in a pitched battle and a dozen raids, has killed one's man in an honourable fashion, and knows a thing or two of strategy and mankind, a certain swagger in the gait is surely to be pardoned. He had put up his horse with due care, and supped with due deliberation; and then, in a very agreeable frame of mind, went out to pay a visit in the grey of the evening. It was not a very wise proceeding on the young man's part. He would have done better to remain beside the fire or go decently to bed. For the town was full of the troops of Burgundy and England under a mixed command; and though Denis was there on safe-conduct, his safe-conduct was like to serve him little on a chance encounter.

It was September 1429; the weather had fallen sharp; a flighty piping wind, laden with showers, beat about the township; and the dead leaves ran riot along the streets. Here and there a window was already lighted up; and the noise of men-at-arms making merry over supper within, came forth in fits and was swallowed up and carried away by the wind. The night fell swiftly; the flag of England, fluttering on the spire-top, grew ever fainter and fainter against the flying clouds – a black speck like a swallow in the tumultuous, leaden chaos of the sky. As the night fell the wind rose, and began to hoot under archways and roar amid the tree-tops in the valley below the town.

Denis de Beaulieu walked fast and was soon knocking at his friend's door; but though he promised himself to stay only a little while and make an early return, his welcome was so pleasant, and he found so much to delay him, that it was already long past midnight before he said good-bye upon the threshold. The wind had fallen again in the meanwhile; the night was as black as the grave; not a star, nor a glimmer of moonshine, slipped through the canopy of cloud. Denis was ill-acquainted with the intricate lanes of Château Landon; even by daylight he had found some trouble in picking his way; and in this absolute darkness he soon lost it altogether. He was certain of one thing only – to keep mounting the hill; for his friend's house lay at the lower end, or tail, of Château Landon, while the inn was up at the head, under the great church spire. With this clue to go upon he stumbled and groped forward, now breathing more freely in open places where there was a good slice of sky overhead, now feeling along the wall in stifling closes. It is an eerie and mysterious position to be thus submerged in opaque blackness in an almost unknown town. The silence is terrifying in its possibilities. The touch of cold window bars to the exploring hand startles the man like the touch of a toad; the inequalities of the pavement shake his heart into his mouth; a piece of denser darkness threatens an ambuscade or a chasm in the pathway; and where the air is brighter, the houses put on strange and bewildering appearances, as if to lead him farther from his way. For Denis, who had to regain his inn without attracting notice, there was real danger as well as mere discomfort in the walk; and he went warily and boldly at once, and at every corner paused to make an observation.

He had been for some time threading a lane so narrow that he could touch a wall with either hand, when it began to open out and go sharply downward. Plainly this lay no longer in the direction of his inn; but the hope of a little more light tempted him forward to reconnoitre. The land ended in a terrace with a bartizan wall, which gave an outlook between high houses, as out of an embrasure, into the valley lying dark and formless several hundred feet below. Denis looked down, and could discern a few tree-tops waving and a single speck of brightness where the river ran across a weir. The weather was clearing up, and the sky had lightened, so as to show the outline of the heavier clouds and the dark margin of the hills. By the uncertain glimmer, the house on his left hand should be a place of some pretensions; it was surmounted by several pinnacles and turret-tops; the round stern of a chapel, with a fringe of flying buttresses, projected boldly from the main block; and the door was sheltered under a deep porch carved with figures and overhung by two long gargoyles. The windows of the chapel gleamed through their intricate tracery with a light as of many tapers, and threw out the buttresses and the peaked roof in a more intense blackness against the sky. It was plainly the hotel of some great family of the neighbourhoood; and as it reminded Denis of a town house of his own at Bourges, he stood for some time gazing up at it and mentally gauging the skill of the architects and the consideration of the two families.

There seemed to be no issue to the terrace but the lane by which he had reached it; he could only retrace his steps, but he had gained some notion of his whereabouts, and hoped by this means to hit the main thoroughfare and speedily regain the inn. He was reckoning without that chapter of accidents which was to make this night memorable above all others in his career; for he had not gone back above a hundred yards before he saw a light coming to meet him, and heard loud voices speaking together in the echoing narrows of the lane. It was a party of men-at-arms going the night round with torches. Denis assured himself that they had all been making free with the wine-bowl, and were in no mood to be particular about safe-conducts or the niceties of chivalrous war. It was as like as not that they would kill him like a dog and leave him where he fell. The situation was inspiriting but nervous. Their own torches would conceal him from sight, he reflected; and he hoped that they would drown the noise of his footsteps with their own empty voices. If he were but silent and fleet he might evade their notice altogether.

Unfortunately, as he turned to beat a retreat, his foot rolled upon a pebble; he fell against the wall with an ejaculation, and his sword rang loudly on the stones. Two or three voices demanded who went there – some in French, some in English; but Denis made no reply, and ran the faster down the lane. Once upon the terrace, he paused to look back. They still kept calling after him, and just then began to double the pace in pursuit, with a considerable clank of armour, and great tossing of the torchlight to and fro in the narrow jaws of the passage.

Denis cast a look around and darted into the porch. There he might escape observation, or – if that were too much to expect – was in a capital posture whether for parley or defence. So thinking, he drew his sword and tried to set his back against the door. To his surprise, it yielded behind his weight; and though he turned in a moment, continued to swing back on oiled and noiseless hinges, until it stood wide open on a black interior. When things fall out opportunely for the person concerned, he is not apt to be critical about the how or why, his own immediate personal convenience seeming a sufficient reason for the strangest oddities and revolutions in our sublunary things; and so Denis, without a moment's hesitation, stepped within and partly closed the door behind him to conceal his place of refuge. Nothing was further from his thoughts than to close it altogether; but for some inexplicable reason – perhaps by a spring or a weight – the ponderous mass of oak whipped itself out of his fingers and clanked to, with a formidable rumble and a noise like the falling of an automatic bar.

The round, at that very moment, debouched upon the terrace and proceeded to summon him with shouts and curses. He heard them ferreting in the dark corners; the stock of a lance even rattled along the outer surface of the door behind which he stood; but these gentlemen were in too high a humour to be long delayed, and soon made off down a corkscrew pathway which had escaped Denis's observation, and passed out of sight and hearing along the battlements of the town.

Denis breathed again. He gave them a few minutes' grace for fear of accidents, and then groped about for some means of opening the door and slipping forth again. The inner surface was quite smooth, not a handle, not a moulding, not a projection of any sort. He got his finger-nails round the edges and pulled, but the mass was immovable. He shook it, it was as firm as a rock. Denis de Beaulieu frowned and gave vent to a little noiseless whistle. What ailed the door? he wondered. Why was it open? How came it to shut so easily and so effectually after him? There was something obscure and underhand about all this that was little to the young man's fancy. It looked like a snare; and yet who could suppose a snare in such a quiet by-street and in a house of so prosperous and even noble an exterior? And yet – snare or no snare, intentionally or unintentionally – here he was, prettily trapped; and for the life of him he could see no way out of it again. The darkness began to weigh upon him. He gave ear; all was silent without, but within and close by he seemed to catch a faint sighing, a faint sobbing rustle, a little stealthy creak – as though many persons were at his side, holding themselves quite still, and governing even their respiration with the extreme of slyness. The idea went to his vitals with a shock, and he faced about suddenly as if to defend his life. Then, for the first time, he became aware of a light about the level of his eyes and at some distance in the interior of the house – a vertical thread of light, widening towards the bottom, such as might escape between two wings of arras over a doorway. To see anything was a relief to Denis; it was like a piece of solid ground to a man labouring in a morass; his mind seized upon it with avidity; and he stood staring at it and trying to piece together some logical conception of his surroundings. Plainly there was a flight of steps ascending from his own level to that of this illuminated doorway; and indeed he thought he could make out another thread of light, as fine as a needle and as faint as phosphorescence, which might very well be reflected along the polished wood of a handrail. Since he had begun to suspect that he was not alone, his heart had continued to beat with smothering violence, and an intolerable desire for action of any sort had possessed itself of his spirit. He was in deadly peril, he believed. What could be more natural than to mount the staircase, lift the curtain, and confront his difficulty at once? At least he would be dealing with something tangible; at least he would be no longer in the dark. He stepped slowly forward with outstretched hands, until his foot struck the bottom step; then he rapidly scaled the stairs, stood for a moment to compose his expression, lifted the arras and went in.

He found himself in a large apartment of polished stone. There were three doors; one in each of three sides; all similarly curtained with tapestry. The fourth side was occupied by two large windows and a great stone chimney-piece, carved with the arms of the Malétroits. Denis recognised the bearings, and was gratified to find himself in such good hands. The room was strongly illuminated; but it contained little furniture except a heavy table and chair or two, the hearth was innocent of fire, and the pavement was but sparsely strewn with rushes clearly many days old.

On a high chair beside the chimney, and directly facing Denis as he entered, sat a little old gentleman in a fur tippet. He sat with his legs crossed and his hands folded, and a cup of spiced wine stood by his elbow on a bracket on the wall. His countenance had a strongly masculine cast; not properly human, but such as we see in the bull, the goat, or the domestic boar; something equivocal and wheedling, something greedy, brutal, and dangerous. The upper lip was inordinately full, as though swollen by a blow or a toothache; and the smile, the peaked eyebrows, and the small, strong eyes were quaintly and almost comically evil in expression. Beautiful white hair hung straight all round his head, like a saint's, and fell in a single curl upon the tippet. His beard and moustache were the pink of venerable sweetness. Age, probably in consequence of inordinate precautions, had left no mark upon his hands, and the Malétroit hand was famous. It would be difficult to imagine anything at once so fleshy and so delicate in design; the taper, sensual fingers were like those of one of Leonardo's women; the fork of the thumb made a dimpled protuberance when closed; the nails were perfectly shaped and of a dead, surprising whiteness. It rendered his aspect tenfold more redoubtable, that a man with hands like these should keep them devoutly folded in his lap like a virgin martyr – that a man with so intense and startling an expression of face should sit patiently on his seat and contemplate people with an unwinking stare, like a god, or a god's statue. His quiescence seemed ironical and treacherous, it fitted so poorly with his looks.

Such was Alain, Sire de Malétroit.

Denis and he looked silently at each other for a second or two.

'Pray step in,' said the Sire de Malétroit. 'I have been expecting you all the evening.'

He had not risen, but he accompanied his words with a smile, and a slight but courteous inclination of the head. Partly from the smile, partly from the strange musical murmur with which the Sire prefaced his observation, Denis felt a strong shudder of disgust go through his marrow. And what with disgust and honest confusion of mind, he could scarcely get words together in reply.

'I fear,' he said, 'that this is a double accident. I am not the person you suppose me. It seems you were looking for a visit; but for my part, nothing was further from my thoughts – nothing could be more contrary to my wishes – than this intrusion.'

'Well, well,' replied the old gentleman indulgently, 'here you are, which is the main point. Seat yourself, my friend, and put yourself entirely at your ease. We shall arrange our little affairs presently.'

Denis perceived that the matter was still complicated with some misconception, and he hastened to continue his explanations.

'Your door ...' he began.

'About my door?' asked the other, raising his peaked eyebrows. 'A little piece of ingenuity.' And he shrugged his shoulders. 'A hospitable fancy! By your own account, you were not desirous of making my acquaintance. We old people look for such reluctance now and then; and when it touches our honour, we cast about until we find some way of overcoming it. You arrive uninvited, but believe me, very welcome.'

'You persist in error, sir,' said Denis. 'There can be no question between you and me. I am a stranger in this countryside. My name is Denis, damoiseau de Beaulieu. If you see me in your house, it is only – '

'My young friend,' interrupted the other, 'you will permit me to have my own ideas on that subject. They probably differ from yours at the present moment,' he added with a leer, 'but time will show which of us is in the right.'

Denis was convinced he had to do with a lunatic. He seated himself with a shrug, content to wait the upshot; and a pause ensued, during which he thought he could distinguish a hurried gabbling as of prayer from behind the arras immediately opposite him. Sometimes there seemed to be but one person engaged, sometimes two; and the vehemence of the voice, low as it was, seemed to indicate either great haste or an agony of spirit. It occurred to him that this piece of tapestry covered the entrance to the chapel he had noticed from without.

The old gentleman meanwhile surveyed Denis from head to foot with a smile, and from time to time emitted little noises like a bird or a mouse, which seemed to indicate a high degree of satisfaction. This state of matters became rapidly insupportable; and Denis, to put an end to it, remarked politely that the wind had gone down.

The old gentleman fell into a fit of silent laughter, so prolonged and violent that he became quite red in the face. Denis got upon his feet at once, and put on his hat with a flourish.

'Sir,' he said, 'if you are in your wits, you have affronted me grossly. If you are out of them, I flatter myself I can find better employment for my brains than to talk with lunatics. My conscience is clear; you have made a fool of me from the first moment; you have refused to hear my explanations; and now there is no power under God will make me stay here any longer; and if I cannot make my way out in a more decent fashion, I will hack your door in pieces with my sword.'

The Sire de Malétroit raised his right hand and wagged it at Denis with the fore and little fingers extended.

'My dear nephew,' he said, 'sit down.'

'Nephew!' retorted Denis, 'you lie in your throat'; and he snapped his fingers in his face.

'Sit down, you rogue!' cried the old gentleman, in a sudden, harsh voice, like the barking of a dog. 'Do you fancy,' he went on, 'that when I had made my little contrivance for the door I had stopped short with that? If you prefer to be bound hand and foot till your bones ache, rise and try to go away. If you choose to remain a free young buck, agreeably conversing with an old gentleman – why, sit where you are in peace, and God be with you.'

'Do you mean I am a prisoner?' demanded Denis.

'I state the facts,' replied the other. 'I would rather leave the conclusions to yourself.'

Denis sat down again. Externally he managed to keep pretty calm; but within, he was now boiling with anger, now chilled with apprehension. He no longer felt convinced that he was dealing with a madman. And if the old gentleman was sane, what, in God's name, had he to look for? What absurd or tragical adventure had befallen him? What countenance was he to assume?

While he was thus unpleasantly reflecting, the arras that overhung the chapel door was raised, and a tall priest in his robes came forth and, giving a long, keen stare at Denis, said something in an undertone to Sire de Malétroit.

'She is in a better frame of spirit?' asked the latter.

'She is more resigned, messire,' replied the priest.

'Now the Lord help her, she is hard to please!' sneered the old gentleman. 'A likely stripling – not ill-born – and of her own choosing, too? Why, what more would the jade have?'

'The situation is not usual for a young damsel,' said the other, 'and somewhat trying to her blushes.'

'She should have thought of that before she began the dance! It was none of my choosing, God knows that: but since she is in it, by our lady, she shall carry it to the end.' And then addressing Denis, 'Monsieur de Beaulieu,' he asked, 'may I present you to my niece? She has been waiting your arrival, I may say, with even greater impatience than myself.'

Denis had resigned himself with a good grace – all he desired was to know the worst of it as speedily as possible; so he rose at once, and bowed in acquiescence. The Sire de Malétroit followed his example and limped, with the assistance of the chaplain's arm, towards the chapel-door. The priest pulled aside the arras, and all three entered. The building had considerable architectural pretensions. A light groining sprang from six stout columns, and hung down in two rich pendants from the centre of the vault. The place terminated behind the altar in a round end, embossed and honeycombed with a superfluity of ornament in relief, and pierced by many little windows shaped like stars, trefoils, or wheels. These windows were imperfectly glazed, so that the night air circulated freely in the chapel. The tapers, of which there must have been half a hundred burning on the altar, were unmercifully blown about; and the light went through many different phases of brilliancy and semi-eclipse. On the steps in front of the altar knelt a young girl richly attired as a bride. A chill settled over Denis as he observed her costume; he fought with desperate energy against the conclusion that was being thrust upon his mind; it could not – it should not – be as he feared.

'Blanche,' said the Sire, in his most flute-like tones, 'I have brought a friend to see you, my little girl; turn round and give him your pretty hand. It is good to be devout; but it is necessary to be polite, my niece.'

The girl rose to her feet and turned towards the newcomers. She moved all of a piece; and shame and exhaustion were expressed in every line of her fresh young body; and she held her head down and kept her eyes upon the pavement, as she came slowly forward. In the course of her advance, her eyes fell upon Denis de Beaulieu's feet – feet of which he was justly vain, be it remarked, and wore in the most elegant accoutrement even while travelling. She paused – started, as if his yellow boots had conveyed some shocking meaning – and glanced suddenly up into the wearer's countenance. Their eyes met; shame gave place to horror and terror in her looks; the blood left her lips; with a piercing scream she covered her face with her hands and sank upon the chapel floor.

'That is not the man!' she cried. 'My uncle; that is not the man!'

The Sire de Malétroit chirped agreeably. 'Of course not,' he said, 'I expected as much. It was so unfortunate you could not remember his name.'

'Indeed,' she cried, 'indeed, I have never seen this person till this moment – I have never so much as set eyes upon him – I never wish to see him again. Sir,' she said, turning to Denis, 'if you are a gentleman, you will bear me out. Have I ever seen you – have you ever seen me – before this accursed hour?'

'To speak for myself, I have never had that pleasure,' answered the young man. 'This is the first time, messire, that I have met with your engaging niece.'

The old gentleman shrugged his shoulders.

'I am distressed to hear it,' he said. 'But it is never too late to begin. I had little more acquaintance with my own late lady ere I married her; which proves,' he added, with a grimace, 'that these impromptu marriages may often produce an excellent understanding in the long-run. As the bridegroom is to have a voice in the matter, I will give him two hours to make up for lost time before we proceed with the ceremony.' And he turned towards the door, followed by the clergyman.

The girl was on her feet in a moment. 'My uncle, you cannot be in earnest,' she said. 'I declare before God I will stab myself rather than be forced on that young man. The heart rises at it; God forbids such marriages; you dishonour your white hair. Oh, my uncle, pity me! There is not a woman in all the world but would prefer death to such a nuptial. Is it possible,' she added, faltering – 'is it possible that you do not believe me – that you still think this' – and she pointed at Denis with a tremor of anger and contempt – 'that you still think *this* to be the man?'

'Frankly,' said the old gentleman, pausing on the threshold, 'I do. But let me explain to you once and for all, Blanche de Malétroit, my way of thinking about this affair. When you took it into your head to dishonour my family and the name that I have borne, in peace and war, for more than threescore years, you forfeited, not only the right to question my designs, but that of looking me in the face. If your father had been alive, he would have spat on you and turned you out of doors. His was the hand of iron. You may bless your God you have only to deal with the hand of velvet, mademoiselle. It was my duty to get you married without delay. Out of pure goodwill, I have tried to find your own gallant for you. And I believe I have succeeded. But before God and all the holy angels, Blanche de Malétroit, if I have not, I care not one jackstraw. So let me recommend you to be polite to our young friend; for upon my word, your next groom may be less appetising.'

And with that he went out, with the chaplain at his heels; and the arras fell behind the pair.

The girl turned upon Denis with flashing eyes.

'And what, sir,' she demanded, 'may be the meaning of all this?'

'God knows,' returned Denis gloomily. 'I am a prisoner in this house, which seems full of mad people. More I know not; and nothing do I understand.'

'And pray how came you here?' she asked.

He told her as briefly as he could. 'For the rest,' he added, 'perhaps you will follow my example, and tell me the answer to all these riddles, and what, in God's name, is like to be the end of it.'

She stood silent for a little, and he could see her lips tremble and her tearless eyes burn with a feverish lustre. Then she pressed her forehead in both hands.

'Alas, how my head aches!' she said wearily – 'to say nothing of my poor heart! But it is due to you to know my story, unmaidenly as it must seem. I am called Blanche de Malétroit: I have been without father or mother for – oh! for as long as I can recollect, and indeed I have been most unhappy all my life. Three months ago a young captain began to stand near me every day in church. I could see that I pleased him; I am much to blame, but I was so glad that any one should love me; and when he passed me a letter, I took it home with me and read it with great pleasure. Since that time he has written many. He was so anxious to speak with me, poor fellow! and kept asking me to leave the door open some evening that we might have two words upon the stair. For he knew how much my uncle trusted me.' She gave something like a sob at that, and it was a moment before she could go on. 'My uncle is a hard man, but he is very shrewd,' she said at last. 'He has performed many feats in war, and was a great person at court, and much trusted by Queen Isabeau in old days. How he came to suspect me I cannot tell; but it is hard to keep anything from his knowledge; and this morning, as we came from mass, he took my hand in his, forced it open, and read my little billet, walking by my side all the while. When he had finished, he gave it back to me with great politeness. It contained another request to have the door left open; and this has been the ruin of us all. My uncle kept me strictly in my room until evening, and then ordered me to dress myself as you see me – a hard mockery for a young girl, do you not think so? I suppose, when he could not prevail with me to tell him the young captain's name, he must have laid a trap for him: into which, alas! you have fallen in the anger of God. I looked for much confusion; for how could I tell whether he was willing to take me for his wife on these sharp terms? He might have been trifling with me from the first; or I might have made myself too cheap in his eyes. But truly I had not looked for such a shameful punishment as this! I could not think that God would let a girl be so disgraced before a young man. And now I have told you all; and I can scarcely hope that you will not despise me.'

Denis made her a respectful inclination.

'Madam,' he said, 'you have honoured me by your confidence. It remains for me to prove that I am not unworthy of the honour. Is Messire de Malétroit at hand?'

'I believe he is writing in the salle without,' she answered.

'May I lead you thither, madam?' asked Denis, offering his hand with his most courtly bearing.

She accepted it; and the pair passed out of the chapel, Blanche in a very drooping and shamefast condition, but Denis strutting and ruffling in the consciousness of a mission, and the boyish certainty of accomplishing it with honour.

The Sire de Malétroit rose to meet them with an ironical obeisance.

'Sir,' said Denis, with the grandest possible air, 'I believe I am to have some say in the matter of this marriage; and let me tell you at once, I will be no party to forcing the inclination of this young lady. Had it been freely offered to me, I should have been proud to accept her hand, for I perceive she is as good as she is beautiful; but as things are, I have now the honour, messire, of refusing.'

Blanche looked at him with gratitude in her eyes; but the old gentleman only smiled and smiled until his smile grew positively sickening to Denis.

'I am afraid,' he said, 'Monsieur de Beaulieu, that you do not perfectly understand the choice I have to offer you. Follow me, I beseech you, to this window.' And he led the way to one of the large windows which stood open on the night. 'You observe,' he went on, 'there is an iron ring in the upper masonry, and reeved through that a very efficacious rope. Now, mark my words: if you should find your disinclination to my niece's person insurmountable, I shall have you hanged out of this window before sunrise. I shall only proceed to such an extremity with the greatest regret, you may believe me. For it is not at all your death that I desire, but my niece's establishment in life. At the same time, it must come to that if you prove obstinate. Your family, Monsieur de Beaulieu, is very well in its way; but if you sprang from Charlemagne, you should not refuse the hand of a Malétroit with impunity – not if she had been as common as the Paris road – not if she were as hideous as the gargoyle over my door. Neither my niece nor you, nor my own private feelings, move me at all in this matter. The honour of my house had been compromised; I believe you to be the guilty person; at least you are now in the secret; and you can hardly wonder if I request you to wipe out the stain. If you will not, your blood be on your own head! It will be no great satisfaction to me to have your interesting relics kicking their heels in the breeze below my windows; but half a loaf is better than no bread, and if I cannot cure the dishonour, I shall at least stop the scandal.'

There was a pause.

'I believe there are other ways of settling such imbroglios among gentlemen,' said Denis. 'You wear a sword, and I hear you have used it with distinction.'

The Sire de Malétroit made a signal to the chaplain, who crossed the room with long silent strides and raised the arras over the third of the three doors. It was only a moment before he let it fall again; but Denis had time to see a dusky passage full of armed men.

'When I was a little younger, I should have been delighted to honour you, Monsieur de Beaulieu,' said Sire Alain; 'but I am now too old. Faithful retainers are the sinews of age, and I must employ the strength I have. This is one of the hardest things to swallow as a man grows up in years; but with a little patience, even this becomes habitual. You and the lady seem to prefer the salle for what remains of your two hours; and as I have no desire to cross your preference, I shall resign it to your use with all the pleasure in the world. No haste!' he added, holding up his hand, as he saw a dangerous look come into Denis de Beaulieu's face. 'If your mind revolts against hanging, it will be time enough two hours hence to throw yourself out of the window or upon the pikes of my retainers. Two hours of life are always two hours. A great many things may turn up in even as little a while as that. And, besides, if I understand her appearance, my niece has still something to say to you. You will not disfigure your last hours by a want of politeness to a lady?'

Denis looked at Blanche, and she made him an imploring gesture.

It is likely that the old gentleman was hugely pleased at this symptom of an understanding; for he smiled on both, and added sweetly: 'If you will give me your word of honour, Monsieur de Beaulieu, to await my return at the end of the two hours before attempting anything desperate, I shall withdraw my retainers, and let you speak in greater privacy with mademoiselle.'

Denis again glanced at the girl, who seemed to beseech him to agree.

'I give you my word of honour,' he said.

Messire de Malétroit bowed, and proceeded to limp about the apartment, clearing his throat the while with that odd musical chirp which had already grown so irritating in the ears of Denis de Beaulieu. He first possessed himself of some papers which lay upon the table; then he went to the mouth of the passage and appeared to give an order to the men behind the arras; and lastly, he hobbled out through the door by which Denis had come in, turning upon the threshold to address a last smiling bow to the young couple, and followed by the chaplain with a hand-lamp.

No sooner were they alone than Blanche advanced towards Denis with her hands extended. Her face was flushed and excited, and her eyes shone with tears.

'You shall not die!' she cried, 'you shall marry me after all.'

'You seem to think, madam,' replied Denis, 'that I stand much in fear of death.'

'Oh no, no,' she said, 'I see you are no poltroon. It is for my own sake – I could not bear to have you slain for such a scruple.'

'I am afraid,' returned Denis, 'that you underrate the difficulty, madam. What you may be too generous to refuse, I may be too proud to accept. In a moment of noble feeling towards me, you forgot what you perhaps owe to others.'

He had the decency to keep his eyes upon the floor as he said this, and after he had finished, so as not to spy upon her confusion. She stood silent for a moment, then walked suddenly away, and falling on her uncle's chair, fairly burst out sobbing. Denis was in the acme of embarrassment. He looked round, as if to seek for inspiration, and seeing a stool, plumped down upon it for something to do. There he sat, playing with the guard of his rapier, and wishing himself dead a thousand times over, and buried in the nastiest kitchen-heap in France. His eyes wandered round the apartment, but found nothing to arrest them. There were such wide spaces between the furniture, the light fell so baldly and cheerlessly over all, the dark outside air looked in so coldly through the windows, that he thought he had never seen a church so vast, nor a tomb so melancholy. The regular sobs of Blanche de Malétroit measured out the time like the ticking of a clock. He read the

25

device upon the shield over and over again, until his eyes became obscured; he stared into shadowy corners until he imagined they were swarming with horrible animals; and every now and again he awoke with a start, to remember that his last two hours were running, and death was on the march.

Oftener and oftener, as the time went on, did his glance settle on the girl herself. Her face was bowed forward and covered with her hands, and she was shaken at intervals by the convulsive hiccup of grief. Even thus she was not an unpleasant object to dwell upon, so plump and yet so fine, with a warm brown skin, and the most beautiful hair, Denis thought, in the whole world of womankind. Her hands were like her uncle's; but they were more in place at the end of her young arms, and looked infinitely soft and caressing. He remembered how her blue eyes had shone upon him, full of anger, pity, and innocence. And the more he dwelt on her perfections, the uglier death looked, and the more deeply was he smitten with penitence at her continued tears. Now he felt that no man could have the courage to leave a world which contained so beautiful a creature; and now he would have given forty minutes of his last hour to have unsaid his cruel speech.

Suddenly a hoarse and ragged peal of cockcrow rose to their ears from the dark valley below the windows. And this shattering noise in the silence of all around was like a light in a dark place, and shook them both out of their reflections.

'Alas, can I do nothing to help you?' she said, looking up.

'Madam,' replied Denis, with a fine irrelevancy, 'if I have said anything to wound you, believe me, it was for your own sake and not for mine.'

She thanked him with a tearful look.

'I feel your position cruelly,' he went on. 'The world has been bitter hard on you. Your uncle is a disgrace to mankind. Believe me, madam, there is no young gentleman in all France but would be glad of my opportunity, to die in doing you a momentary service.'

'I know already that you can be very brave and generous,' she answered. 'What I *want* to know is whether I can serve you – now or afterwards,' she added, with a quaver.

'Most certainly,' he answered, with a smile. 'Let me sit

beside you as if I were a friend, instead of a foolish intruder; try to forget how awkwardly we are placed to one another; make my last moments go pleasantly; and you will do me the chief service possible.'

'You are very gallant,' she added, with a yet deeper sadness ... 'very gallant ... and it somehow pains me. But draw nearer, if you please; and if you find anything to say to me, you will at least make certain of a very friendly listener. Ah! Monsieur de Beaulieu,' she broke forth – 'ah! Monsieur de Beaulieu, how can I look you in the face?' And she fell to weeping again with a renewed effusion.

'Madam,' said Denis, taking her hand in both of his, 'reflect on the little time I have before me, and the great bitterness into which I am cast by the sight of your distress. Spare me, in my last moments, the spectacle of what I cannot cure even with the sacrifice of my life.'

'I am very selfish,' answered Blanche. 'I will be braver, Monsieur de Beaulieu, for your sake. But think if I can do you no kindness in the future – if you have no friends to whom I could carry your adieux. Charge me as heavily as you can; every burden will lighten, by so little, the invaluable gratitude I owe you. Put it in my power to do something more for you than weep.'

'My mother is married again, and has a young family to care for. My brother Guichard will inherit my fiefs; and if I am not in error, that will content him amply for my death. Life is a little vapour that passeth away, as we are told by those in holy orders. When a man is in a fair way and sees all life open in front of him, he seems to himself to make a very important figure in the world. His horse whinnies to him; the trumpets blow and the girls look out of window as he rides into town before his company; he receives many assurances of trust and regard – sometimes by express in a letter – sometimes face to face, with persons of great consequence falling on his neck. It is not wonderful if his head is turned for a time. But once he is dead, were he as brave as Hercules or as wise as Solomon, he is soon forgotten. It is not ten years since my father fell, with many other knights around him, in a very fierce encounter, and I do not think that any one of them, nor so much as the name of the fight is now remembered. No, no, madam, the nearer you come to it, you see that death is a dark and dusty corner, where a man gets into his tomb and has the door shut after him till the judgment day. I have few friends just now, and once I am dead I shall have none.'

'Ah, Monsieur de Beaulieu!' she exclaimed, 'you forget Blanche de Malétroit.'

'You have a sweet nature, madam, and you are pleased to estimate a little service far beyond its worth.'

'It is not that,' she answered. 'You mistake me if you think I am so easily touched by my own concerns. I say so, because you are the noblest man I have ever met; because I recognise in you a spirit that would have made even a common person famous in the land.'

'And yet here I die in a mousetrap – with no more noise about it than my own squealing,' answered he.

A look of pain crossed her face, and she was silent for a little while. Then a light came into her eyes, and with a smile she spoke again.

'I cannot have my champion think meanly of himself. Any one who gives his life for another will be met in Paradise by all the heralds and angels of the Lord God. And you have no such cause to hang your head. For ... Pray, do you think me beautiful?' she asked, with a deep flush.

'Indeed, madam, I do,' he said.

'I am glad of that,' she answered heartily. 'Do you think there are many men in France who have been asked in marriage by a beautiful maiden – with her own lips – and who have refused her to her face? I know you men would half despise such a triumph; but believe me, we women know more of what is precious in love. There is nothing that should set a person higher in his own esteem; and we women would prize nothing more dearly.'

'You are very good,' he said; 'but you cannot make me forget that I was asked in pity and not for love.'

'I am not so sure of that,' she replied, holding down her head. 'Hear me to an end, Monsieur de Beaulieu. I know how you must despise me; I feel you are right to do so; I am too poor a creature to occupy one thought of your mind, although, alas! you must die for me this morning. But when I asked you to marry me, indeed, and indeed, it was because I respected and admired you, and loved you with my whole soul, from the very moment that you took my part against my uncle. If you had seen yourself, and how noble you looked, you would pity rather than despise me. And now,' she went on, hurriedly checking him with her hand, 'although I have laid aside all reserve and told you so much, remember that I know your sentiments towards me already. I would not, believe me, being nobly born, weary you with importunities into consent. I too have a pride of my own; and I declare before the holy mother of God, if you should now go back from your word already given, I would no more marry you than I would marry my uncle's groom.'

Denis smiled a little bitterly.

'It is a small love,' he said, 'that shies at a little pride.'

She made no answer, although she probably had her own thoughts.

'Come hither to the window,' he said, with a sigh. 'Here is the dawn.'

And indeed the dawn was already beginning. The hollow of the sky was full of essential daylight, colourless and clean; and the valley underneath was flooded with a grey reflection. A few thin vapours clung in the coves of the forest or lay along the winding course of the river. The scene disengaged a surprising effect of stillness, which was hardly interrupted when the cocks began once more to crow among the steadings. Perhaps the same fellow who had made so horrid a clangour in the darkness not half-an-hour before, now sent up the merriest cheer to greet the coming day. A little wind went bustling and eddying among the tree-tops underneath the windows. And still the daylight kept flooding insensibly out of the east, which was soon to grow incandescent and cast up that red-hot cannon-ball, the rising sun.

Denis looked out over all this with a bit of a shiver. He had taken her hand, and retained it in his almost unconsciously.

'Has the day begun already?' she said; and then, illogically enough: 'the night has been so long! Alas! what shall we say to my uncle when he returns?'

'What you will,' said Denis, and he pressed her fingers in his.

She was silent.

'Blanche,' he said, with a swift, uncertain, passionate utterance, 'you have seen whether I fear death. You must know well enough that I would as gladly leap out of that window into the empty air as lay a finger on you without your free and full consent. But if you care for me at all do not let me lose my life in a misapprehension; for I love you better than the whole world; and though I will die for you blithely it would be like all the joys of Paradise to live on and spend my life in your service.'

As he stopped speaking, a bell began to ring loudly in the interior of the house; and a clatter of armour in the corridor showed that the retainers were returning to their post, and the two hours were at an end.

'After all that you have heard?' she whispered, leaning towards him with her lips and eyes.

'I have heard nothing,' he replied.

'The captain's name was Florimond de Champdivers,' she said in his ear.

'I did not hear it,' he answered, taking her supple body in his arms, and covered her wet face with kisses.

A melodious chirping was audible behind, followed by a beautiful chuckle, and the voice of Messire de Malétroit wished his new nephew a good morning.

Scar Tissue

by HENRY S. WHITEHEAD

What 'is your opinion on the Atlantis question?' I asked my
friend Dr Pelletier of the U.S. Navy, as he relaxed during the
afternoon swizzle hour on my West Gallery. He waved a depre-
cating hand.

'All the real evidence points to it, doesn't it, Canevin? The
harbor here in St Thomas, for instance. Crater of a volcano.
What could bring a crater down to sea-level like that, unless the
submergence of quadrillions of tons of earth and rock, or the
submergence of a continent?' Then: 'What made you ask me
that, Canevin?'

'A case,' I replied. 'Picked him up yesterday morning just
after he had jumped ship from that Spanish tram, the *Bilbao*,
that was coaling at the West India Docks yesterday morning.
She pulled out this afternoon without him. Says his name is
Joe Smith. A rough and tough bird, if I ever saw one. Up
against it. They were crowding him pretty heavily, according
to his story. Extra watches. Hazing. Down with the damned
gringo! Looks as if he could handle himself, too – hard as nails.
I've got him right here in the house.'

'What are you keeping him shut up for?' inquired Pelletier
lazily. 'There isn't anybody on his trail now, is there?'

'No,' I said. 'But he was all shot to pieces from lack of sleep.

31

Red rims around his eyes. He's upstairs, asleep, probably dead to the world. I looked in on him an hour ago.'

'What bearing has the alleged Joe Smith on Atlantis?' Pelletier's tone was still lazily curious.

'Well,' I said, 'Smith looks to me as though he had one of those dashes of "ancestral memory", like the fellow Kipling tells about, the one who "remembered" being a slave at the oars, and how a Roman galley was put together. Only, this isn't any measly two thousand years ago. This is – '

Pelletier straightened in his lounge-chair.

'Good God, Canevin! And he's here – in this house?'

Twenty minutes later Smith stepped out on the gallery. He looked vastly different from the beachcomber I had picked up near the St Thomas market-place the morning before. He was tall and spare, and my white drill clothes might have been made for him. He was cleanly shaven and his step was alert.

Pelletier did most of the talking. He established a quick footing with Smith with an obvious view to getting his story of the 'buried memory' which the fellow had mentioned to me, and which pointed, he had hinted, at Atlantis.

At the end of ten minutes or so, Pelletier surprised me.

'What was your college, Smith?' he inquired.

'Harvard, and Oxford,' he answered. 'Rhodes Scholar. Took my M.A. at Balliol. Yes, of course, Dr Pelletier. Ask me anything you like. This "buried memory" affair has come on me three different times, as a matter of fact. Always when I'm below par physically, a bit run down, vitality lower than normal. I mentioned it to Mr Canevin yesterday – sensed that he would be interested. I've read his stuff, you see, for the past dozen years or so!'

I was getting interested myself now.

'Tell us about it,' invited Pelletier, and Joe Smith proceeded to do so:

'It began when I was a small boy, after scarlet fever. I got up too soon and went swimming, had a relapse, and the next three or four days lying in bed, I "realised" that I was *memoriter familiar* with a previous life in which I wore clothing of animal skins and used stone-headed clubs. I had the ability to run long distances and go up and down trees without much effort, and could easily club a bear to death. The thing passes off, dims out, although the recollection remained quite clear, as soon as I was well again.

'The second time was after the Spring track-meet with Yale when I was twenty-one. I had run in the 220, and then, half an hour later, I put everything I had into a quarter-mile, and won it. I lay around and rested according to my trainer's orders for a week – not even reading a book. Then I "remembered" – not the cave-life this time – but Africa. Portuguese and Negroes; enormous buildings, some of them with walls sixteen feet thick. Granite quarries and the Portuguese sweating the Blacks in some ancient gold mines. There were two rivers. I fished in them a great deal, with a big iron hook. They were called, the rivers, I mean, the Lindi and the Sobi.

'Curious kind of place. There was one enormous ruin, a circular tower on top of a round hill which was formed by an outcropping in the granite. There was a procession of bulls carved around the pediment. Yes, and the signs of the Zodiac.'

Southern Rhodesia!' I cried out. 'The Portuguese controlled it in the Fifteenth Century, before Columbus' time. Why, man, that place is the traditional site of Solomon's gold mines!'

'Right!' Smith remarked, turning an intelligent eye in my direction. 'It was pronounced in those days – "Zim-baub-weh" – accent on the first syllable. I've often wondered if it wasn't the Romans who carved those bulls, they had the place first, called it *Anaeropolis*. Plenty of legionaries were Mithraists, and the bull was Mithras' symbol, you know.'

'And the last one, Smith,' Pelletier cut in. 'You mentioned Atlantis, Canevin tells me.'

'Well,' began Smith once more, 'the fact that it was Atlantis is, really secondary. There is one item in *that* "memory" which is of very much greater interest, I should imagine.

'I don't want to be theatrical, gentlemen! But – well, I think the best way to begin telling you it is to show you this.'

He rose and loosened his belt, pulled up his shirt and singlet, exposing a bronzed torso. Beginning a half-inch above his right hip-bone and extending straight across as though laid out with a ruler across the abdomen, ran a livid, inch-wide scar, cut to eventually form scar-tissue.

Joe Smith tucked in his shirt, tightened his belt, and sat down again. 'That's where it begins,' he said, and, as my house-man, Stephen Penn, appeared at this moment with the dinner-cocktails, he added: 'I'll tell you about it after dinner.'

It was Pelletier who started things off as soon as we were settled on the gallery again, with coffee and Chartreuse before us.

'I want to know, please, how you happen to be alive.'

Smith smiled wryly.

'I never told this before,' he said, 'and if I was somewhat preoccupied during dinner it was because I've been figuring out how to put it all together for you.

'It's hard to put into words but it seemed as if I were walking through a short enclosed passageway, rather wide, stone-flagged, and low-ceilinged. In front of me, beside me, and behind me, walked eighteen or twenty others, all of us armed. Up in front of us, in bronze armor, and closing our rear, marched eight legionaries of the Ludektan army assigned to us as guards.

'We came out into the drenching sunlight of a great sanded arena. We followed our advance guard in a sharp turn to the right and wheeled to the right-face before a great awninged box full of the Ludektan nobles and dignitaries, where we saluted.

'Do you get that picture? Here we were, prisoners of war – after a couple of months of the hardest training I have ever known, in the Ludektan gladitorial school, about to shed our blood to make an Atlantean holiday!

'The really tough part of it was the uncertainty. I mean a fellow might be paired to fight one of his friends. But I was fortunate that day. I was paired with a Gamfron – a nearly black Atlantean mountain lion, an animal about the size and heft of an Indian black panther – Bagheera, in Kipling's Mowgli yarn! I had been armed with a short, sharp, double-edged sword and a small bronze buckler. Otherwise I had been given choice of my own accoutrement and I had selected greaves, a light breast-plate and a close-fitting helmet with a face-guard attachment with eye holes, covering practically my whole face and the back and sides of my neck.

'When it came to my turn to step out on the sand and wait for the lion to be released, I asked the official in charge for permission to discard the buckler and use an additional weapon, a long dagger, in my left hand. I received the permission, and at the signal-blast which was made with a ram's horn, walked slowly towards the cage-entrance. I had noted that the sun was shining directly, full against that particular iron door.

'My strategy worked precisely as I had hoped.

The great beast came out blinking. Before its cat eyes became adjusted to the sun's glare I launched myself upon it, and when I sprang away, the hilt of that dagger was sticking in the Gamfron's back. The beast rolled over in the sand, hoping, I suppose, to dislodge the dagger. The hilt was twisted, I noticed, when the Gamfron again crouched for its leap at me.'

'In the split seconds before it launched itself at me I could hear the wild tumult from the stands. The crowd swayed hysterically – screaming for blood. Mine.

'I side-stepped as the beast charged, but instead of trying another slash, I whirled, and as the beast plowed up the sand beside me, I threw myself upon it and thrust my sword into the soft flesh of its throat, severing the jugular. Then, my feet and legs wedged hard under the animal's flanks. I reached under its jaws, swinging backward from the fulcrum of my knees and hauled the Gamfron's head backwards towards me.

'The snap could be heard throughout the arena. The great beast relaxed under me. I recovered my sword, stood up, placed my right foot upon the carcass and held up my sword toward the notables in a rigid salute.

'The next thing I was directly conscious of was a hand falling on my left shoulder. I relaxed, let down my sword, and heard the voice of the official in charge of the gladiators telling me that I was reprieved. I stumbled along beside him around the edge of the arena under a continuous shower of felt hats and gold and silver coin until I felt the grateful shade of a stone passage-way on my almost melting back, and a minute later, with my armor off, I was being doused from head to foot with buckets of cold water.

'It was perhaps twenty minutes later when the official in charge of the gladiators came into the small stone-flagged room where I was tying the thongs of my sandals.

'The people demand your presence in the arena,' he announced from just inside the doorway. I rose and bowed in his direction. A public gladiator in the Ludekta had the status of a slave. Then the official announced: "You have been chosen to fight Godbor as the day's concluding event – come!"

'Half way along the passageway the official turned to me, whispering with earnestness and vehemency directly into my ear. And when he had finished I was a new man! Gone now were all the feelings of rebellious hatred which his announcement at the rubbing-room door had raised up in me. He turned and led the way out into the arena. And I followed him now, gladly, eagerly, my head up and my heart beating high.

'A thunderous roar greeted us, and the massed thousands rose in their seats like one man. A black slave stepping towards us from the barrier handed a bulging leather sack to the official. He took it and spoke to me over his shoulder. "These are your coins that were thrown into the ring. I will keep them safely for you".

'Then we proceeded to a point directly before the great can-

35

opied enclosure of the nobles. Here, after saluting with my arms and hands straight up above my head and not giving their spokesman an opportunity to address me, I put into immediate effect what my unsuspecting friend had whispered in my ear.

'I will fight Godbor to the death,' I shouted.

'A deafening howl went up from the multitude. I waited quietly until the tumult died and then as soon as I could be heard once more I addressed the nobles.

' "My Lords, I have proclaimed my willingness to please you despite the Ludektan Law which requires no man to fight twice in the arena on the same day. I beseech your nobility therefore, in return for this my good will to meet your desire, that you accord me my liberty, if I survive."

'There was a deathly silence about the arena, while the nobles consulted together.

'I stood there, rigid, waiting for this decision which meant far more than life or death to me. I could see the right arms of the members of that vast concourse being raised in the Ludektan voting gesture of approval.

'Then, as Bothon, who had been generalissimo of all the Ludektan armies, rose in his place to give me my answer, that sharp humming sound stilled and died and twenty thousand men and women leaned forward on their benches to hear the decision. Bothon was both terse and explicit.

'The petition is granted,' he announced.

'Remembering clearly all that the arena official had told me, I waited once more until I could be heard, and when that instant arrived I saluted the nobles and said:

' "I would gladly slay the traitorous dog Godbor without reward, o illustrious, for not even yourselves, who deprived him of his Ludektan citizenship and condemned him to the arena, are better aware of his infamy than we of Lemuria who refused to profit by his treachery. I petition you that the rules which are to govern our combat be stated here, in his presence and mine, that there be no treachery but a fair fight."

'At this, which had been listened to in a dead silence that was almost painful, the mob on the benches broke out again. Watching the nobles' enclosure I saw Bothon turning his eyes to those about him. When he had gathered their decisions he turned to me and made the sign of approval.

Back in the preparation rooms with the chief official himself over-looking every detail, I got myself ready for my last fight in the arena. I was very well aware that I was now confronted with the most serious ordeal of my life. Not only had I spent most of my strength in that conflict with the wild beast, but also I was about to encounter in the traitor Godbor, one of the most skillful and tricky hand-to-hand fighters that the Ludektan army had ever produced. He would be fresh, too.

'At high noon, Godbor who had been similarly prepared in another room, walked beside me in the usual form of procession, proceeding through the passageway and into the blinding glare, shortly to stand side by side listening to Bothon repeat the rules of the combat.

'And then on a great square of freshly pressed and dampened sand we two stood facing each other tensed for a conflict which one or the other would never leave.

'At the single blast from the herald's horn I leaped at my enemy. He had started forward at the same instant himself. I caught his descending blade squarely on the knop of my bronze buckler, relaxing my left arm to lessen the shock of the blow, at the same time delivering a thrust above Godbor's buckler. The fresh-ground razor-like point of my sword struck his upper shoulder, severing the tendon and rendering his left arm useless. I made a rapid recovery, but the equally swift forward leap of Godbor brought him breast to breast with me. He managed to shift his sword into a dagger-like position, and I was barely able to divert the stabbing stroke which he aimed for my left side.

'We backed away from each other then for, according to the stated rules of the combat, our initial attack-and-defence was completed. Then I lowered my sword as I saw Godbor drooping forward, his knees sagging under him, his eyes closing. As I stood there, waiting for him to recover himself, he suddenly dropped off the buckler from his left arm, and, launching himself forward, drove the bronze helmet he wore against my chest.

'I went crashing down under the terrific blow and I could hear very clearly, rising above everything, the howl of rage which rose from the spectators on every side.

'Then, Godbor was upon me, his face a distorted mask of hatred. His sword slashed into my right hip bone and across the lower and unprotected edge of my ribs.

'A dull-red cloud descended upon me, and a vicious stab of pain that swelled with each second. My fast-dimming eyes caught the edge of the strange spectacle of the people of the benches leaping down on the sand in their dozens and scores and hundreds, pouring over the barriers into the arena like cascades.

'And, with the dimming chorus of their massed roars of hate in my ears, I let go of life.'

Joe Smith ceased speaking, rose, and walked over to the centre table. I noticed that his hands trembled as he poured himself out the second drink he had taken since he had been in my house. Deep lines, too, that had not shown before dinner, were in his clean-shaven face. It was evident that the telling of his strange tale had done something to him. He settled in his chair again before either Pelletier or I offered any comment.

'I imagine Godbor didn't survive you very long,' I said. 'That mob probably took him apart.'

Smith nodded. 'He was very unpopular – execrated, in fact.'

Pelletier's comments were in an entirely different vein.

'I beg of you, don't misunderstand me, Smith, but most people would say it's a wonderful yarn, as a yarn, but that's all. Atlantis, Zimbabwe, that cave-boy stuff! That scar of yours for a point of departure; well-known facts, open to any reader, about the ancestral memory theory; and all of 'em worked up into a yarn that is, I grant you, a corncracker! Exactly right, you see, for a couple of fellows like Canevin and me, known to be interested in out-of-the ordinary matters. That, I say, is what the majority of people would say. I'm not insulting you by putting it that way myself. I merely call attention to the fact that there isn't a thing in it that couldn't have been put together by a clever story-teller.'

Smith merely nodded. 'Precisely as you put it,' he said. 'Precisely, except for this.'

And he rose from his chair, once again loosened his belt, and exposed that frightful scar.

Pelletier, the surgeon uppermost at once, got up, came over to Smith, and peered closely at it.

'H'm,' he remarked, 'the real mystery isn't in that yarn, Smith. It's in how you ever survived this! The breadth of this scar shows that the wound must have been several inches deep. It cut straight through the intestines and just about bisected the spleen. Such a cut would kill a man in a few minutes.'

'It did, as I told you,' said Smith, a little crisply.

'My dear man!' protestingly, from Pelletier.

But Joe Smith remained entirely unruffled.

'You know, of course, what scar-tissue feels like to the touch,' he said. 'Run your hand over this, Doctor. Then tell us if you ever felt any other scar-tissue like it. It *looks* like any other scar, of course.'

Pelletier did as requested, his attitude plainly sceptical. But he straightened up from the examination with a very different look on his face.

'Good God!' he breathed. 'There's nothing to feel! This thing only *looks* like scar tissue! What – ?'

Smith carefully tucked in his shirt.

'It's precisely the way I told it to you. I was born without any appearance of a scar, although it falls within the classification of so-called "birth-marks". It did not begin to appear until I was twenty-seven. That was my age when I died there in the arena, from that wound in the same place, just as I told you.'

Pelletier looked at Joe Smith in blank silence. Then he asked, 'Did you have it on you during those two other "memory-experiences" you spoke of, as a cave boy, or there in Africa in the Fifteenth Century?'

'No,' Smith replied. 'I suppose the reason is that I was not yet twenty-seven years of age in either of those two experiences.'

'Well, I'll take your word for it all, Smith,' said Pelletier. 'It's been mighty interesting.'

The two of them bowed to each other, Pelletier smiling whimsically, Joe Smith's tired, lined face inscrutable.

Just after this Pelletier took his departure.

Half an hour later – it must have been about eleven – Smith rapped on the door of my bedroom. He was in pajamas and bathrobe, and wearing a pair of my spare slippers.

'Would you like to hear the rest of it?' he asked, coming in and taking a chair. He placed something he had been carrying beside him on the wide chair's cushion.

'There isn't much more of it,' he remarked, 'but I'd rather like you to hear it all together.'

'Fire away,' I invited, settling myself.

'That "birth-mark" of mine,' he began, 'isn't the only thing I could have shown you this evening. I had *this* around my waist, too!'

He reached down beside him and unrolled the thing he had brought into my room. It was a pigskin money-belt.

'There's between seven and eight hundred pounds in this,' he remarked, laying it on the table beside him, 'in Bank of England notes. I thought you might put it in your safe until tomorrow, and then I'll put it in the bank. And now, here's the rest of my story.

'I'd been on board the *Bilbao* nearly two months when we struck this port of St Thomas to coal. It was, to be precise, the fourteenth of August when I went on board her, in Santander. Three days before that, while I was sitting eating my dinner, a big fellow came in and took a table across the room from me. I didn't particularly take note of him except that he was big. He had an ugly face that seemed vaguely familiar.

'Then quite suddenly, it broke upon me. I knew who he was!

It was "Godbor", Canevin – Godbor to the life! The man who had killed me in the arena!

'I sat there, and just sweated. I remembered putting my face between my hands, my elbows on the table, and feeling just plain sick.

'And then he moved over to my table and sat down.

'He was civil enough. His name was Fernando Lopez. He was the first mate of the *Bilbao*, just arrived in Santander harbor, expecting to clear for Buenos Aires three or four days from then.

'Lopez proposed that we eat together. Somehow I couldn't refuse. There was almost a weird fascination about the man. While we ate I told him I was a painter and required as much time to myself, including mealtime, as I could get. I spoke, of course, without trying to insult him, but nevertheless giving the impression I wanted to be alone. But it was no use.

'We drank together, and within a few hours I had passed out. When I awoke it was morning – the morning of the day the *Bilbao* was to clear from Santander, about seven o'clock. And then I found my money-belt gone! Fernando Lopez, too, was gone! He had probably gone on board, I figured, ready for the ship's departure, confident that he had made a clean getaway.'

'He saw me, as soon as I came on board. I charged him flatly with the theft. He made no bones about it, admitted he had taken the money-belt from me after I passed out, and had it down in his cabin. I demanded its return and he shrugged, walking toward his cabin.

'As I walked in after him, something struck me over the head. I came to in a berth, with my hands ironed; and a head that seemed too big for my body.

'For three days I sweated through a period that was like a nightmare.

'The captain, an old man named Chico Perez, who was Lopez' uncle, forced me to sign on. I was watched every minute and given the work of two men to do.

'They ironed me again the day we put into Buenos Aires. Lopez was taking no chances on my jumping ship and reporting him. Then, two days after we cleared from there, the old captain disappeared. I have no doubts in my own mind about what happened to him. Lopez probably threw him overboard.

'That fact I imagine, saved me. You see, the entire crew had sailed with the old man, who was a part owner of the ship. Lopez, while he now commanded the *Bilbao*, did not dare to risk mutiny if another member of the ship's company "disappeared" in the same manner.

'We made four or five other South American ports, Cartagena last of all, and then we were put in to St Thomas for coal. This was the first American port of the voyage. I picked up a little hope.

'We were actually in sight of St Thomas when I got my chance. It was about five o'clock in the evening, four days ago. I was on deck, and we had just made our landfall. Lopez was coming towards me across the deck. I waited until he was within a few feet of me, and then I lunged forward. My fist hit Lopez' jaw, knocking him flat on the deck.

'He was up almost instantly, snarling, and a knife appeared in his hand. I ducked his first rush and tripped him as he swept by me. His knife clattered on the deck as he hit it.

'I lunged forward and my fingers closed over the blade. I don't know what happened next, but suddenly the knife was imbedded in Lopez' back and I was on my feet, trembling with a cold sweat.

'One by one the crew members walked up. They all seemed to be smiling at me.

'I watched the knife being withdrawn from Lopez' body by one of them, and then, five men quietly heaved the body overboard.

'Nothing was said to me. There was no report, no investigation after we anchored in St Thomas Harbor.

'I had gone straight down to Lopez' cabin after the moneybelt, put it on, and came back on deck.

'No one stopped me when I went ashore. I imagine that that ship's family was only too glad to get rid of the fellow who had relieved them of Fernando Lopez. The rest of it you know, Canevin. I might add that I haven't the smallest possible regret over killing Lopez. If those "ancestral memories" of mine are authentic, I have killed before, but never in *this life*, certainly.'

Joe Smith sat silent, and I sat across from behind him and looked at him. The only thing I could think of to ask, seemed an incongruity after what I had listened to that day! However I had to ask it.

'What is your real name Smith?' I inquired.

He stared at me.

'Joe Smith,' he said.

I nodded then. 'I'll put your money in the safe and we'll go to the bank with it in the morning.'

I saw him out, and picked up the money-belt from the table

and carried it over to my house-safe standing in the corner of my bedroom.

I opened the safe and was about to lay the belt inside when I felt something rough against my hand. I turned it about and looked. A name was embossed upon the fine pigskin leather of the other side. I held it up to the light to read it. I read:

'JOSEPHUS TROY SMITH'

I put the belt inside and closed and locked the safe.

Then I came back and sat down in the chair where I had listened to my guest's recital of his recent adventure aboard the Spanish tramp steamer *Bilbao*.

Josephus Troy Smith. It wasn't so vastly different from 'Joe Smith', and yet what a different viewpoint that full name had given me! Josephus Troy Smith, America's foremost landscapist Josephus Troy Smith! I recalled now whom I was having the honor of entertaining here in my house on Denmark Hill, St Thomas, Virgin Islands of the U.S.A. He was an eccentric artist, Josephus Troy Smith – or was he . . .

Through the Veil

Sir Arthur Conan Doyle

He was a great shock-headed, freckle-faced Borderer, the lineal descendant of a cattle-thieving clan in Liddesdale. In spite of his ancestry he was as solid and sober a citizen as one would wish to see, a town councillor of Melrose, an elder of the Church, and the chairman of the local branch of the Young Men's Christian Association. Brown was his name – and you saw it printed up as 'Brown and Handiside' over the great grocery stores in the High Street. His wife, Maggie Brown, was an Armstrong before her marriage, and came from an old farming stock in the wilds of Teviothead. She was small, swarthy, and dark-eyed, with a strangely nervous temperament for a Scotch woman. No greater contrast could be found than the big tawny man and the dark little woman, but both were of the soil as far back as any memory could extend.

One day – it was the first anniversary of their wedding – they had driven over together to see the excavations of the Roman Fort at Newstead. It was not a particularly picturesque spot. From the northern bank of the Tweed, just where the river forms a loop, there extends a gentle slope of arable land. Across it run the trenches of the excavators, with here and there an exposure of old stonework to show the foundations of the ancient walls. It had been a huge place, for the camp was fifty acres in extent, and the fort fifteen. However, it was all made easy for them since Mr. Brown knew the farmer to whom the land belonged. Under his guidance they spent a long summer evening inspecting the trenches, the pits, the ramparts, and all the strange variety of objects which were waiting to be transported to the Edinburgh Museum of Antiquities. The buckle of a woman's belt had been dug up that very day, and the farmer was discoursing upon it when his eyes fell upon Mrs. Brown's face.

'Your good leddy's tired,' said he. 'Maybe you'd best rest a wee before we gang further.'

Brown looked at his wife. She was certainly very pale, and her dark eyes were bright and wild.

'What is it, Maggie? I've wearied you. I'm thinkin' it's time we went back.'

'No, no, John, let us go on. It's wonderful! It's like a dreamland place. It all seems so close and so near to me. How long were the Romans here, Mr Cunningham?'

'A fair time, mam. If you saw the kitchen midden-pits you would guess it took a long time to fill them.'

'And why did they leave?'

'Well, mam, by all accounts they left because they had to. The folk round could thole them no longer, so they just up and burned the fort aboot their lugs. You can see the fire marks on the stanes.'

The woman gave a quick little shudder. 'A wild night – a fearsome night,' said she. 'The sky must have been red that night – and these grey stones, they may have been red also.'

'Aye, I think they were red,' said her husband. 'It's a queer thing, Maggie, and it may be your words that have done it; but I seem to see that business aboot as clear as ever I saw anything in my life. The light shone on the water.'

'Aye, the light shone on the water. And the smoke gripped you by the throat. And all the savages were yelling.'

The old farmer began to laugh. 'The leddy will be writin' a story aboot the old fort,' said he. 'I've shown many a one ower it, but I never heard it put so clear afore. Some folk have the gift.'

They had strolled along the edge of the foss, and a pit yawned upon the right of them.

'That pit was fourteen foot deep,' said the farmer. 'What d'ye think we dug oot from the bottom o't? Weel, it was just the skeleton of a man wi' a spear by his side. I'm thinkin' he was grippin' it when he died. Now, how cam' a man wi' a spear doon a hole fourteen foot deep. He wasna' buried there, for they aye burned their dead. What make ye o' that, mam?'

'He sprang doon to get clear of the savages,' said the woman.

'Weel, it's likely enough, and a' the professors from Edinburgh couldna gie a better reason. I wish you were aye here, mam, to answer a' oor deeficulties sae readily. Now, here's the altar that we foond last week. There's an inscreeption. They tell me it's Latin, and it means that the men o' this fort give thanks to God for their safety.'

They examined the old worn stone. There was a large deeply-cut 'VV' upon the top of it.

'What does "VV" stand for?' asked Brown.

'Naebody kens,' the guide answered.

'*Valeria Victrix*,' said the lady softly. Her face was paler than ever, her eyes far away, as one who peers down the dim aisles of over-arching centuries.

'What's that?' asked her husband sharply.

She started as one who wakes from sleep. 'What were we talking about?' she asked.

'About this "VV" upon the stone.'

'No doubt it was just the name of the Legion which put the altar up.'

'Aye, but you gave some special name.'

'Did I? How absurd! How should I ken what the name was?'

'You said something – "*Victrix*," I think.'

'I suppose I was guessing. It gives me the queerest feeling, this place, as if I were not myself, but someone else.'

'Aye, it's an uncanny place,' said her husband, looking round with an expression almost of fear in his bold grey eyes. 'I feel it mysel'. I think we'll just be wishin' you good evening', Mr. Cunningham, and get back to Melrose before the dark sets in.'

Neither of them could shake off the strange impression which had been left upon them by their visit to the excavations. It was as if some miasma had risen from those damp trenches and passed into their blood. All the evening they were silent and thoughtful, but such remarks as they did make showed that the same subject was in the minds of each. Brown had a restless night, in which he dreamed a strange connected dream, so vivid that he woke sweating and shivering like a frightened horse. He tried to convey it all to his wife as they sat together at breakfast in the morning.

'It was the clearest thing, Maggie,' said he. 'Nothing that has ever come to me in my waking life has been more clear than that. I feel as if these hands were sticky with blood.'

'Tell me of it – tell me slow,' said she.

'When it began, I was oot on a braeside. I was laying flat on the ground. It was rough, and there were clumps of heather. All round me was just darkness, but I could hear the rustle and the breathin' of men. There seemed a great multitude on every side of me, but I could see no one.

There was a low chink of steel sometimes, and then a number of voices would whisper "Hush!" I had a ragged club in my hand, and it had spikes o' iron near the end of it. My heart was beatin' quickly, and I felt that a moment of great danger and excitement was at hand. Once I dropped my club, and again from all round me the voices in the darkness cried, "Hush!" I put oot my hand, and it touched the foot of another man lying in front of me. There was some one at my very elbow on either side. But they said nothin'.

'Then we all began to move. The whole braeside seemed to be crawlin' downwards. There was a river at the bottom and a high-arched wooden bridge. Beyond the bridge were many lights – torches on a wall. The creepin' men all flowed towards the bridge. There had been no sound of any kind, just a velvet stillness. And then there was a cry in the darkness, the cry of a man who has been stabbed suddenly to the hairt. That one cry swelled out for a moment, and then the roar of a thoosand furious voices. I was runnin'. Every one was runnin'. A bright red light shone out, and the river was a scarlet streak. I could see my companions now. They were more like devils than men, wild figures clad in skins, with their hair and beards streamin'. They were all mad with rage, jumpin' as they ran, their mouths open, their arms wavin', the red light beatin' on their faces. I ran, too, and yelled out curses like the rest. Then I heard a great cracklin' of wood, and I knew that the palisades were doon. There was a loud whistlin' in my ears, and I was aware that arrows were flyin' past me. I got to the bottom of a dyke, and I saw a hand stretched doon from above. I took it, and was dragged to the top. We looked doon, and there were silver men beneath us holdin' up their spears. Some of our folk sprang on to the spears. Then we others followed, and we killed the soldiers before they could draw the spears oot again. They shouted loud in some foreign tongue, but no mercy was shown them. We went ower them like a wave, and trampled them doon into the mud, for they were few, and there was no end to our numbers.

'I found myself among buildings, and one of them was on fire. I saw the flames spoutin' through the roof. I ran on, and then I was alone among the buildings. Some one ran across in front o' me. It was a woman. I caught her by the arm, and I took her chin and turned her face so as the light of the fire would strike it. Whom think you that it was, Maggie?'

His wife moistened her dry lips. 'It was I,' she said.

He looked at her in surprise. 'That's a good guess,' said he. 'Yes, it was just you. Not merely like you, you understand. It was you – you yourself. I saw the same soul in your frightened eyes. You looked white and bonny and wonderful in the firelight. I had just one thought in my head – to get you awa' with me; to keep you all to mysel' in my own home somewhere beyond the hills. You clawed at my face with your nails. I heaved you over my shoulder, and I tried to find a way oot of the light of the burning hoose and back into the darkness.

'Then came the thing that I mind best of all. You're ill, Maggie. Shall I stop? My God! you have the very look on your face that you had last night in my dream. You screamed. He came runnin' in the firelight. His head was bare; his hair was black and curled; he had a naked sword in his hand, short and broad, little more than a dagger. He stabbed at me, but he tripped and fell. I held you with one hand, and with the other – '

His wife had sprung to her feet with writhing features.

'Marcus!' she cried. 'My beautiful Marcus! Oh, you brute! you brute! you brute!' There was a clatter of tea-cups as she fell forward senseless upon the table.

They never talk about that strange isolated incident in their married life. For an instant the curtain of the past had swung aside, and some strange glimpse of a forgotten life had come to them. But it closed down, never to open again. They live their narrow round – he in his shop, she in her household – and yet new and wider horizons have vaguely formed themselves around them since that summer evening by the crumbling Roman fort.

CHARLES DICKENS

Charles John Huffam Dickens was born in Landport, Portsmouth in 1812. When he was ten years old, his family settled in Camden Town, a poor neighbourhood of London. A defining moment in the young Dickens' life came only two years later, when his father – the inspiration for the character of Mr Micawber in *David Copperfield* – was imprisoned in the Marshalsea debtor's prison. As a result, Dickens was sent to Warren's blacking factory, where he worked in appalling conditions and gained a first-hand acquaintance with poverty. After three years Dickens resumed his education, but the experience was highly formative for him, and would later be fictionalised in both *David Copperfield* and *Great Expectations*.

Dickens' writing career began in around 1830, when he started to write for the journals *The Mirror of Parliament* and *The True Sun*. Three years later, he became parliamentary journalist for *The Morning Chronicle*, and also began to have some successes with his fiction: His first short story, A 'Dinner at Popular Walk', appeared in the *Monthly Magazine* in December of 1833, and his first book, a collection titled *Sketches by Boz*, was published in 1836. However, his real breakthrough came in 1837, with the serialised publication of *Posthumous Papers of the Pickwick Club* – the work was hugely popular, and transformed Dickens into a well-known literary figure.

Over the next few years, at an almost incredible rate, Dickens wrote *Oliver Twist* (1837-39), *Nicholas Nickleby* (1838-39) and *The Old Curiosity Shop* and *Barnaby Rudge* (1840-41). In 1842, he travelled with his wife to the United States and Canada (where he gave lectures denouncing slavery), and in the years following produced his five 'Christmas Books'. During the fifties, after brief spells living in Italy and Switzerland, he continued to write at a seemingly inexhaustible pace, producing some of his best work: David Copperfield (1849-50), Bleak House (1852-53), Hard Times (1854), Little *Dorrit* (1857), *A Tale of Two Cities* (1859), and *Great Expectations* (1861).

During the latter stages of his life, Dickens turned his focus from writing to giving readings. In 1869, during one such reading, he collapsed, showing symptoms of a mild stroke. He died at home one year later, aged 58. He was buried in the Poets' Corner of Westminster Abbey, where the inscription on his tomb reads: "He was a sympathiser to the poor, the suffering, and the oppressed; and by his death, one of England's greatest writers is lost to the world." Dickens is now regarded as the greatest writer of the Victorian era, and one of the greatest English authors since Shakespeare.

ROBERT LOUIS STEVENSON

Robert Lewis Balfour Stevenson was born in Edinburgh, Scotland in 1850. Aged seventeen, he enrolled at the University of Edinburgh, but he was a disinterested student whose bohemian lifestyle detracted from his studies, and four years later, in April of 1971, he declared his decision to pursue a life of letters. A keen traveller, Stevenson became involved with a number of European literary circles, and had his first paid piece, an essay entitled 'Roads', published in 1873.

Stevenson suffered from various ailments and a "weak chest" for the whole of his life, and spent much of his adult years searching for a place of residence suitable to his state of ill health. In 1880, he married Fanny Van de Grift, and they moved between France, Britain and California together. It was during these years that Stevenson produced much of his best-known work – *Treasure Island,* in 1883,

The Strange Case of Dr Jekyll and Mr Hyde, in 1886, and *Black Arrow,* in 1888. Following the death of his father in 1887, Stevenson devoted his later years to travels in the Pacific. During the late 1880s, he spent extended periods of time in both the Hawaiian and Samoan Islands, befriending many native and colonial leaders of the day and writing a number of accounts of his travels. In 1890 he purchased a 400-acre tract of land in Samoa, where he would remain for the rest of his life.

By 1894, still suffering from various ailments, he fell into a state of depression, and in December of that year, while straining to open a bottle of wine, he collapsed, most likely from a cerebral haemorrhage. A few hours later he was dead, aged just 44. Stevenson remains highly popular to this day, and is ranked the 26th most translated author in the world.

HENRY S. WHITEHEAD

Henry St. Clair Whitehead was born in New Jersey in 1882. He graduated from Harvard University in 1904, having been in the same class as future American president Franklin D. Roosevelt, and was ordained as a deacon in Episcopal Church in 1912. Between 1921 and 1929 he served as acting archdeacon of the Virgin Islands, where he gathered much of the material he was to use in his speculative fiction. An early correspondent of fellow writer H. P. Lovecraft, Whitehead's stories appeared from 1924 onwards in *Weird Tales* and a number of other pulp magazines. His 1944 collection, *Jumbee and Other Uncanny Tales*, is regarded as a classic of horror literature. Whitehead spent his later life in Dunedin, Florida, and died in 1932, aged 50.

SIR ARTHUR CONAN DOYLE

Arthur Conan Doyle was born in Edinburgh, Scotland, in 1859. It was between 1876 and 1881, while studying medicine at the University of Edinburgh, that he began writing short stories, and his first piece was published in *Chambers's Edinburgh Journal* before he was 20. In 1882, Conan Doyle opened an independent medical practice in Southsea, near Portsmouth. It was here, while waiting for patients, that he turned to writing fiction again, composing his first novel, *The Narrative of John Smith*.

In 1887, Conan Doyle's first significant work, *A Study in Scarlet*, appeared in *Beeton's Christmas Annual*. It featured the first appearance of detective Sherlock Holmes, the protagonist who was to eventually make Conan Doyle's reputation. A prolific writer, Conan Doyle continued to produce a range of fictional works over the following years. In 1893, feeling that the character of Sherlock Holmes was distracting him from his historical novels, he had Holmes apparently plunge to his death in the short story 'The Final Problem'. However, eight years later, following a public outcry from his readers, Conan Doyle 'resurrected' the detective in what is now widely regarded as his *magnum opus, The Hound of the Baskervilles.*

Sherlock Holmes went on to feature in fifty-six short stories and four novels, cementing Conan Doyle's reputation as probably the most famous crime writer of all time. Aside from his fiction, Conan Doyle was also a passionate political campaigner – a pamphlet he published in 1902, defending the United Kingdom's much-criticised role in the Boer War, is seen as a major contributor to his receiving of a knighthood in that same year.

In his later years, following the death of his son in World War I, Conan Doyle became deeply interested in spiritualism and psychic phenomena, producing several works on the subjects and engaging in a very public friendship and falling out with the American magician Harry Houdini. He died of a heart attack while living in East Sussex in 1930, aged 71.

www.ingramcontent.com/pod-product-compliance
Lightning Source LLC
Chambersburg PA
CBHW030534020726
47494CB00004B/1364